Laddy

Amazing
Animal stories
based on true events

Laddy

Amazing
Animal stories
based on true events

Imprint:

©2024 Laddy GbR

Cover design, production and
publishing:
BoD - Books on Demand, Norderstedt

Cover picture:

Photo: Pixabay

love-for-animals-2479736_1920

Pixabay License: https://pixabay.com/de/service/license/

ISBN: 978-3-7597-2256-0

Animals can't write the word love,
but they can show it all the better.

Unknown author

6

Table of Contents

The Siberian Wolf Pack

Not many people can say they are willing to sacrifice themselves for the good of another person. Especially not for someone they don't even know. That makes the story of Siberian forestry inspector Sergei all the more incredible. Because he was saved by wild animals, a pack of wolves, who were willing to sacrifice themselves for him.

Dimitri was born into a Siberian family of railway workers. The village where he lived was far from the big city of Irkutsk, and the railroad was not only the largest employer in the area, but also the only one. At least if you were looking for a secure job. You could still choose whether you wanted to be a mechanic or a train driver.

After Dimitri finished school, he first tried his luck in faraway Irkutsk, where he began to study engineering.

After only a few months, he realized that the big city was too much for him. So the young man followed the family tradition and became a train driver, just like his father and his father's father. A new dream was born. His goal was to become one of the train drivers on the most famous railroad in the world. Dimitri wanted to travel the 9,288 kilometers from Moscow to Vladivostok in the cab of the Trans-Siberian Railway.

After successfully completing his training, he began driving as a second engineer on various routes, and after a short time was assigned to drive freight trains as a first engineer. This was the first step towards his goal.

Dimitri loved his job and enjoyed driving through the vast Siberian countryside in winter and summer, transporting his heavy cargo from city to city. On each trip he melted into the vastness, beauty, and also the loneliness of the sheer endlessness of Siberia. The young man liked both the hot, short summers and the icy, long winters. For him, Siberia was the most beautiful and adventurous country in the world.

Dimitri was enthusiastic about his current route. The route was never the same, and no matter how many times he traveled it, he always discovered new places of beauty.

One day, however, he would experience something he would never forget for the rest of his life.

It is difficult to capture the wild beauty of Siberia in a few words. At about 16 million square kilometers, the country is larger than Europe, and from north to south, polar desert, tundra, taiga, forest steppe, and steppe follow one another. Countless wild animals live in the vast primeval forests. Unfortunately, there are far too few forest rangers to protect these animals from poachers. The life of these poorly paid men is meager, dangerous and lonely. Wandering around the country, you will often see graves with inscriptions that tell you which ranger fell victim to one or more poachers.

One of these brave forest rangers was Sergei. He dedicated his life to nature and animals more than 40 years ago. The forest inspector lived far from civilization in a state-owned log cabin in the middle of the forests near Lake Baikal. The nearest village was a two-day hike away, and it took Sergei four to five days to get to Irkutsk. Fortunately, he only had to go to the city once a year.

The forest inspector loved the silence and the wilderness. He took care of the animals, studied their behavior, respected them and hunted their human enemies, the poachers. He was the master of the forest, he knew every tree, every path, every hill and every danger spot. He could move silently and make himself invisible. Sergei was feared by the poachers, and since he had captured the two most dangerous of them a few years ago and put them in prison, his territory was avoided by all poachers.

The forester didn't hate the days when he had to go to the village, but he didn't like them much either. They were simply necessary to replenish his supplies and send his monthly report to the office in town. He used the fax machine in the village store.

He also got everything he needed to live here. Beans, bacon, tea, pipe tobacco, rifle cartridges, and his beloved vodka. Sergei finished every evening with a glass of vodka. He swore that this was the secret of his robust health. He couldn't remember ever having been to a doctor. Except for the dentist, of course. He went to the dentist when he visited the city. A glass of vodka. No more, no less. When the bottle was empty, he knew it was time to make the report and go to the village.

People liked the oddball, who looked like a wild hermit, a kind of Robinson Crusoe from the woods. His shaggy hair was hidden under a fur cap. The long, gray beard covered much of his face. He looked grumpy, and those who didn't know him gave him a wide berth when he stepped out of the woods, dragging his sled and shouldering his rifle. Those who knew him were delighted, because Sergei always had a funny story to tell.

It was always the same. As soon as he reached the edge of the village, he was quickly surrounded by children. Laughing and dancing around him, they shouted: "Father Sergei, tell us a story about wolves or bears."

The forest ranger usually adjusted his fur hat, scratched his long gray beard, and smiled before beginning his story. His story always ended when he entered the village store, where he gave each child a treat.

As she did every month, the store owner, Ludmilla, stood behind the counter and packed up Sergei's things while he stood at the fax machine and sent off his report. The two of them chatted and when everything was done, the forest inspector paid. As usual, Ludmilla took the bills, put them in the cash register and put the change on the table.

She had taken over the small shop from her parents a few years ago and had known Sergei since childhood. Her speech was the same. "Father Sergei, how much longer are you going to live out there in the forest? Shouldn't you have retired by now?"

The forester put away the groceries and slipped the two rubles in change into his pocket. The tone of Ludmilla's voice caught his attention. He noticed the worry lines on her forehead. "Well," he cleared his throat, "this was supposed to be my last year, but I've asked the comrades in charge for an extension. I think I can easily work for another five years."

Ludmilla closed the register. "You know you are very welcome here in the village. My uncle's small apartment recently became available. He's moved to the city for good. It doesn't cost much in rent and..."

14

"Child," Sergei interrupted her, "I belong in the forest and I feel safe in my log cabin."

They were silent for a moment. Then Sergei added, "Now tell me what's wrong. I can see it on your face. It's not about my retirement."

She nodded. "I read it in the paper," she began in a hushed voice, "they were fired."

"Who?"

"The Osmanov brothers. You put them in jail four years ago."

Sergei nodded. "Yes. They were two tough guys. I caught them red-handed. One of them even pointed at me and pulled the trigger, but his shotgun jammed. When I said my gun would work and pointed it at them, they surrendered." His expression darkened. "They had a lot of furs in their hideout. The sentence for both of them was still far too lenient."

Ludmilla agreed. Sergei made a dismissive gesture with his hand and turned to leave. "I hope they learned their lesson during their imprisonment."

Ludmilla spoke louder. "They swore revenge then," she warned.

Sergei went to the door and opened it. A cold wind blew into the village shop. He turned around for a moment. "Child, don't worry. You don't want to go back to prison. There haven't been any poachers in this area since the two brothers were locked up. That was a deterrent."

As soon as he had finished speaking, he trudged to the sled, tied up his purchases and set off. He no longer heard Ludmilla's "Good luck, Father Sergei."

Sergei had mastered the art of setting up camp for the night in the freezing cold. Instead of building a snow cave, he decided to spend the night in a snow ditch. Without much effort, he dug a hole in the snow and built a fire. He had carried some dry wood on his sled just for this purpose. He stretched a canvas tent over the hole for a roof and used a large fur for insulation on the cold ground.

The forest ranger added two large logs to the crackling fire before curling up in his sleeping bag, also made of furs. Wolves howled in the distance. Somewhere a branch collapsed under the weight of the snow. For Sergei, these were everyday sounds. He was tired and fell asleep.

A sharp pain rudely woke the forester from his sleep. Someone had pushed something hard into his side. A punch in the face and a kick in the ribs followed. Sergei instinctively raised his arms to protect his head from further blows. A cry escaped his lips: "Ahh...". His side hurt like hell. Broken ribs. He blinked, recognized two figures, and started to turn around to grab his weapon.

Malicious laughter rang out. "Looking for this, old man?" one of the men asked.

"Go on, shoot him!" demanded the second man.

A surge of adrenaline ran through Sergei. It was unmistakably the Osmanov brothers. The two poachers must have seen him in the village and followed his trail.

Goose bumps formed on the back of his neck and spread down his back to the tips of his toes.

"What do you want?" he hissed. Inwardly, he cursed himself. In the past, this would not have happened. His sleep had always been so light that he had even heard animals approaching. How could this have happened? If only he had listened to Ludmilla's warning. His life was about to end. Ended by two criminals who were going to kill a bunch of wild animals to sell their furs. Or who killed bears to sell their paws, so coveted in China. Anger boiled over. Sergei's right hand moved almost imperceptibly to his belt. His knife was there. He would defend himself. He could not allow these two men to continue poaching.

"No, not here. He should suffer. He should know that he will die and wait for death, just as we have waited in prison for four years for the day of his release".

A wolf's howl broke the silence. More wolves joined in.

One of the brothers laughed and pointed into the dark night. "They're singing your death song!"

The butt of the rifle slammed into Sergei's head. The last sound he heard was the wolves' howling, which grew louder and louder.

When Sergei came to, the sun had risen. He looked straight into the yellowish eyes of a wolf. Fear ran through him. Sergei opened his mouth to scream, but no sound came out. His puff of breath intersected with the animal's. The wolf stood calmly in front of him, staring at him. No snarling, no hasty movement, no growling. It just stood there, staring at him. The look was almost gentle.

Sergei thought he was suffering from delusions. It must have something to do with the blow on the head, he told himself. The inspector tried to move. He immediately winced in pain. The two poachers had broken at least one or two of his ribs. They dug into his side like lances. He was also lying on something very hard, and his head was throbbing terribly. When he tried to move his arms and legs, he realized that he was handcuffed to the railing with iron chains. Sergei raised his head as high as he could and was scared to death.

There were at least ten or twelve wolves around him. The animals he had protected for four decades would soon kill and eat him. He hoped for a quick death bite so he wouldn't feel the pain when they ate him alive. Sergei was terrified. Deadly afraid.

For a moment, he wished that the poachers had shot him. Then he would lie in the forest and feel nothing. Now he had to surrender to his fate. He was at the mercy of the wolf pack.

Serguei closed his eyes for a moment. He decided to bend his head as far back as possible to expose his neck for a merciful death bite. The wolf in front of him approached and sniffed. He could feel its hot breath on his face. The whole body of the bound and wounded man trembled.

"Now bite," he whispered, staring into the wolf's eyes again. Again he saw no aggression in the animal. His gaze moved along the wolf. It was a female wolf. He recognized a large scar on the right front paw. Memories flashed through his mind. "Is that you?" he asked the wolf, as if she could answer him. It had to be her. It was the young wolf he had rescued from a poacher's trap years ago and nursed back to health.

He undoubtedly recognized the she-wolf he had fed on raw meat until she regained her strength and disappeared into the forest one day.

Sergei knew that wolves use their howling as a social call. They howl into the night and use it to announce their location in order to learn the locations of other wolves. The howl warns of enemies and calls for hunting. It warns the pack and serves to emphasize the strategic hierarchy of the pack.

Usually the lead wolf or pair of lead wolves begins the howling, and other wolves join in with the howling of the alpha. The howling of the wolves was the last sound he heard before he was knocked unconscious. Had she called her pack because he was in danger?

Sergei tried to look around as best he could. The wolves had surrounded him and were mostly sitting or lying in the track bed.

Had they really gathered to help him? He couldn't believe it. Touched in his heart that a pack of wild wolves was protecting him from other wild animals, the forest ranger still knew that he was going to die. He was lying on railroad tracks, and freight trains passed by every day. And even if they didn't come, he would freeze to death during the night. His fate was sealed. The poachers wanted him to face his death helplessly, and that was exactly what would happen.

Sergei lost all sense of time. Surrounded by a pack of wolves, he just lay there and waited. The trembling with fear was replaced by shivering with cold.

Finally, the time had come. It sounded as if the tracks began to hum. A freight train weighing tens of thousands of tons was approaching. Sergei looked into the eyes of the she-wolf, who had demonstratively placed herself next to him. "Now go on!" he breathed in a weak voice.

Dimitri loved the ride into the early morning. When the fog lifted and the sun made the frost glisten silvery on the trees beside the tracks, the white landscape shone like the treasure chamber of the legendary Ice Queen.

It was pleasantly warm in the cab. Enjoying the view, he slowed the freight train slightly on a long curve and unscrewed his thermos. Half a minute later he took his first sip of tea. The engineer put the cup down and concentrated on the track. A little later he recognized something on the track.

"An obstacle," he muttered and slowed down again. "What is it?"

Dimitri looked at the obstacle. It was animals. "Wolves!" he groaned and blew the train whistle to startle the pack.

They must have found a dead animal on the tracks and were feeding there. The young engineer could think of no other explanation, so he blew the whistle again, and the shrill, loud sound echoed several times.

The animals did not move. Dimitri wondered what to do. The rules forbade him to stop, should he ignore them?

Even when he tried to shoo the pack away again with a long whistle, there was no reaction. Instinctively, without thinking about the rules, he hit the brakes. The wheels locked and the wagons, weighing several tons, slid over the rails with a squeak. The wolves did not even move when the train came dangerously close to the pack. Deadly afraid, they sat or stood on the rails and stared at the locomotive.

Dimitri noticed that they had gathered around something. It was as if they were forming a ring. He was afraid to drive into the group and closed his eyes.

At last. The freight train had stopped. The distance to the pack of wolves was less than ten meters. Dimitri could hardly believe what he saw. A man was lying on the tracks. Did the wolves see him as prey?

He waited. The wolves did not move. Then he saw the lead wolf sniff the face of the man lying on the tracks, turn and run off into the woods. All the other wolves followed. The driver waited two or three minutes to see if the pack came back, then got out. He rushed to the man and found that Sergei was chained to the tracks. The driver immediately got tools and freed the injured forester.

As he brought him to the locomotive, the wolves let out a howl. A smile crossed Sergei's face. The wolves he had been protecting from poachers for four decades, like other animals, had saved his life. They formed a living shield that was visible from afar. Without this living wall, Sergei would have been run over by Dimitri's freight train. The wolves in the pack had risked their lives for the forest inspector.

The fisherman and the shark

Many people are afraid of sharks. This is mainly due to the fact that these animals are often portrayed as monsters. Reports of shark attacks make sensational headlines and sell well, especially in the print media.

Although the fate of the swimmers or surfers involved is truly terrible, such reports unfortunately reflect a false image of these animals. The attacks on humans are primarily the result of the shark mistaking them for its natural prey, a seal.

The often quoted comparison that more people die each year from falling coconuts than from shark attacks is not scientifically proven, but it does show that shark attacks are rather rare.

Like all marine life, sharks suffer greatly from marine pollution. They get caught in old fishing nets or die from eating plastic or microplastics. Sharks have lived on this earth for millions of years and are threatened with extinction due to human-induced marine pollution.

Sharks are not cuddly and they are dangerous. No one should swim or surf in waters where sharks hunt. It is their habitat and people should respect it.

The following story is about one of the most extraordinary friendships that has ever existed. The friendship between a great white shark, one of the most dangerous of its kind along with the tiger and hammerhead sharks, and a human.

Australia attracts many tourists every year with its sunny weather and white beaches. They come to enjoy the sun and sea, to swim, dive and surf. On many beaches, certain areas are fenced off with nets to prevent possible encounters between swimmers and sharks.

Fishing boats cruise the deep blue ocean off the coast of Australia. The warm and temperate waters are rich in fish species and promise good catches.

Arnold Pointer and the sea were one and the same. The Australian was a passionate fisherman and loved his job, which was also his greatest hobby. Arnold was out on the boat almost every day.

His skin was tanned, his face weathered. A well-worn captain's hat covered his short hair. The fisherman was popular, and his friendly demeanor occasionally brought him a few paying tourists to take out on the water for a tour. The euros and dollars were an easy extra income.

Like every other day, Arnold set sail that day. But this day would change his life. The sea was calm and there were many boats in the harbor due to the holiday. Aside from the usual swimmers and tourist cruises, the sea would remain free of competition.

"Wonderful!" he shouted to the harbormaster as he walked across the dock to his Little Molly. "The fish are just waiting for me today."

Joe Miller shook his head with a grin. "Arnold, you're the happiest man I know. Tell me, when are you ever in a bad mood?"

Arnold stopped, turned around, held out his right hand, and pointed to the sea with a slight twist. "I guess the day I realize I can never go outside again."

Joe winked. "That's going to take a few years. Good catch."

"Thanks."

The engine started for the first time, and "Little Molly" set course for the open sea. The warm wind blew into the 35-year-old captain's face. It felt like a gentle caress. The small boat glided playfully over the sea. The sun reflected on the water in thousands of glittering dots, and every now and then a dolphin would jump out of the deep blue to dive back into the sea with its long beak.

Arnold reached his fishing spot, slowed down and cast the net. Then, as he did every day after casting the net, he let his thoughts drift. Today he was thinking about going back to his favorite waterfront tavern for the evening. There he was often approached by tourists who wanted to go out to sea for a few dollars. It was always easy money for Arnold. That is, if the tourists didn't bombard him with questions or start drinking and partying on board.

"They pay well," he muttered, and decided to invite three or four of them again. He did a quick mental calculation and would charge each of them 25 Australian dollars for the trip. That included a bottle of water and a packed lunch that he would pack himself. That was a profit of 20 dollars per person for him.

After a few more brainstorming sessions on how to make more money from tourists, he went to work.

Arnold was happy as he left for his home port. He had had better days, but also much worse. Herring gulls circled his ship. He picked up speed. The engine roared and the bow of his fishing boat glided through the gentle waves. As he neared the shore, the fisherman noticed something strange. The water was foaming. Something was tugging violently at the safety net stretched out in the water to protect swimmers from sharks.

Arnold slowed down and steered the boat to the spot. The fisherman was certain that someone there needed his help. He reached over and grabbed the binoculars. There was no lifeguard. His eyes circled.

"Nobody noticed anything," he said to himself and put the binoculars down.

He walked slowly to the spot in question. The water was really boiling. There was nothing to be seen on the surface. Either a diver or a large fish had become entangled in the safety net.

Maybe a dolphin, he thought. A diver couldn't create such a violent whirlpool.

Skillfully, the experienced fisherman slowed the boat down completely and turned it sideways. It swam gently toward the spot. The captain jumped at the sight. Instinctively, he held on. There was no diver or dolphin wriggling in the net. A shark was entangled. Not just any shark, but a great white shark.

One of the most dangerous predators in the ocean. The fisherman was sure it was a female. The shark was at least five and a half meters long, and at up to seven meters, female great whites were considerably longer than the males, whose size was limited to four to five meters.

Razor-sharp teeth flashed at the captain. The stocky body twisted wildly. The captured animal flapped its powerful tail fin. While its back and flanks were light gray, its belly was completely white.

Arnold knew this was a dangerous animal, but also an endangered one. Great whites are critically endangered and protected in Australia.

There is no question that this species of shark can be extremely dangerous to humans, but humans are not its prey. Sharks are curious and often explore interesting things by poking or biting. The latter, of course, can be fatal to humans.

"I know we're in your territory and not the other way around," Arnold said to the shark. Of course, he knew the predator could not hear or understand him, but it did the fisherman good, and most importantly, it calmed him down. His nervousness and fear of the shark vanished.

"We pulled the net so we humans wouldn't hit you sharks."

He got an overview. The huge white shark was mercilessly entangled in the net and would die a miserable death without help. The captain knew what he had to do. Even though he made his living fishing, and great whites were not popular here near the beach, he would help him. He felt a real obligation to do so. "The sea feeds us both," he shouted, turning around. He feverishly looked around the small fishing boat, trying to figure out how to help the predator out of the net.

The quickest way would be to take the knife and jump into the water. A few cuts would free the shark. Arnold grinned a little at the thought. "...and I would be in mortal danger."

So using a knife was out of the question. At the same time, he had an idea that quickly took shape. In a straight line, Arnold fetched the long pole with the hook that he used to pull various things out of the sea. He grabbed his sharp fishing knife and attached it to the other end of the hooked pole with a piece of string and tape. The boat rocked back and forth. The huge sea beast was fighting for its life. The water frothed. A glance over the side of the boat followed, then Arnold let the pole slide into the water and began to cut the net. The shark suddenly calmed down. The struggling and twisting stopped in a split second. The huge shark lay still. It was as if it was watching what the fisherman was doing. The great white seemed to sense that it was being helped.

Arnold had heard that you could put sharks into a kind of stupor by closing their mouths and turning them around. There was no question in his mind that this method might work on a small baby shark, but not on this adult animal weighing up to 1,100 pounds. The mouth was wide and long. Between 23 and 28 teeth in the upper jaw and between 20 and 26 teeth in the lower jaw were waiting for a powerful bite.

After the shark lay motionless in the water for a while, visibility improved. Arnold recognized the net in the clear water and cut it piece by piece. After a few minutes, he was able to free the shark.

What happened next would change fisherman Arnold Pointer's life forever.

"Done!" he shouted triumphantly, pulling the pole out of the water. His eyes were fixed on the great white. The female shark swam away, but not away. It circled Arnold's boat and stopped. After a few minutes, the captain smiled, waved goodbye, and muttered to himself: "So long, baby, I gotta get going."

He started the engine and headed for the coast. He radioed that the net had been cut. That section of beach would be closed until it was repaired.

What happened next was unbelievable. The shark did not swim away. It followed the boat and circled it without attacking. Arnold felt like he had a dog with him.

It was only when the boat docked in the harbor that the white shark disappeared.

When Arnold went out to sea again over the next few days, it didn't take long for the shark lady to swim alongside his boat. She accompanied him out to sea and stayed next to the boat until he returned to port.

It was as if the shark wanted to thank the fisherman. The predator could not be separated from the boat. The fisherman was touched at first, but when he realized that the shark lady would not leave his side of the boat, he realized that he had to change something in his life. She was, of course, preventing him from catching fish. The sea creatures fled the predator.

Arnold befriended the great white shark. The shark even jumped out of the water and let the fisherman stroke its head for a moment. It was like a hunter playing with his dog. The shark had become Arnold's extraordinary pet. This friendship between a shark and a human is probably unique in history.

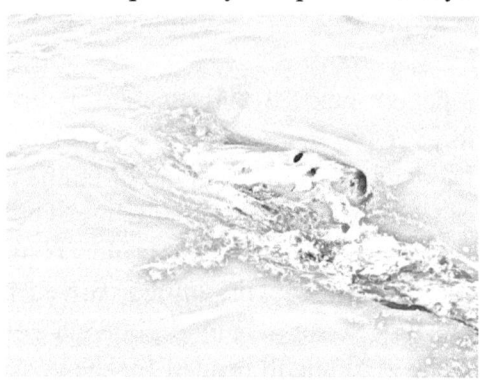

The former fisherman no longer earns his money from fishing, but from tourists. Some of them check in on his boat or go out to sea in support boats when the crowds are big and follow Arnold.

They see the shark's fin on almost every trip, but sometimes they are lucky enough to witness the unique spectacle of the large marine predator jumping out of the water close to the edge of the boat and being patted on the head by its rescuer.

Arnold may have lost his fishing, but he has found a friendship for life.

Horse Love

This story is set in Morocco. The country is officially called the Kingdom of Morocco and is located in northwestern Africa.

It is separated from the European mainland only by the Strait of Gibraltar. The first Berber tribes settled in what is now Morocco in ancient times. Romans settled in the coastal region around the birth of Christ, before the Vandals invaded and the country was Islamized by Arabs in the 7th century.

The most famous cities are Casablanca, Fez, Rabat, Tangier and Agadir.

Today, only 0.1% of Moroccans are Christians. One of them is Salim, whose special experience I would like to share with you today.

Why I am telling you about Salim's Christian faith will become clear at the end of the story.

(Roman archaeological site)   *(Strait of Gibraltar - overlooking from Africa to Europe)*

Salim's ancestors had always been farmers and horse breeders. The family property was not far from the city. In addition to cattle, sheep and goats, the family bred the ancient Arabian Berber horse with great success.

Salim was also born with an incredible love for animals. He learned how to handle animals from his grandparents and parents and was taught a wealth of knowledge about them. Even as a young boy, Salim had a preference for horses. He helped deliver foals, mucked out the stables, and cared for the animals when they were healthy and when they were sick. He learned quickly, willingly and a lot. In the western world today he would probably be called a "horse whisperer". Salim loved the horses and they loved him.

Animals are so incredible that we humans often don't give them credit for how great they are. One of their most underrated qualities is their ability to form strong bonds with people.

When Salim's parents grew old and passed the farm on to him, the experienced man focused on horse breeding. Not only did he breed and sell Berber horses, but he also took in old and sick horses. His father was skeptical at first, but his son's success proved him right. Salim's reputation had grown to the point where he was able to make a living from breeding horses.

His sanctuary for old animals had also grown considerably. He even saved some animals from being euthanized and nursed them back to health against all the vets' hopes. Of course, this didn't always work, which is why Salim was so happy every time he succeeded. Weeks later, when an animal that had been declared terminally ill was running around the paddock, he thanked God for the miracle. That was the reward that made him happy. The horse farmer couldn't get enough of frolicking horses. As they galloped across the vast pastures, their manes blowing in the warm wind, his heart laughed.

Salim had just turned 48 when he crossed paths with a very special horse. In the meantime, the shrewd horse breeder had also established himself as a businessman. Being a Christian in a Muslim country was not easy. But Salim's friendly and honest manner, coupled with his expertise in horses, was in demand and rewarded. After the death of his parents, he set up a wholesale business for horse feed and riding accessories in addition to the horse breeding and sanctuary. Salim had many regular customers and was known, appreciated and loved in his community as well as in the surrounding towns.

On the day it all began, he was sitting in his office doing paperwork. He organized invoices, made a few phone calls, and was thrilled to receive a large order over the phone. A smile crossed Salim's face. He had been courting this major customer for a long time. Now the time had come. His offer was preferred over the competition. The order volume would increase by more than 20 percent starting next month.

"This is a reason to celebrate," he said to himself.

His eyes wandered past the various trophies and certificates hanging on the wall to the large wall clock. It was almost closing time.

The office was a side room of the large store. The businessman entered the sales area through a side door, scurried through the shelves to the cash register, and caught a few glimpses of a conversation between a customer and his sales clerk. He heard only the words: "Foal, euthanize, sick!"

Salim got goosebumps, paused for a moment, and approached the two men. He introduced himself politely. "Salam Aleikum," he greeted them and immediately spoke. "Sorry to interrupt the conversation, but I overheard something in passing about a foal and euthanasia. Can I get some background information?"

The customer, an elderly gentleman, was not particularly attractive to Salim. He was wearing a linen djellaba caftan and leather sandals. Ray Ban sunglasses were pushed up over his thinning gray hair. An expensive Rolex watch gleamed on his left wrist. Salim didn't care if it was real or fake. The only thing that bothered him was the ostentatious display. The customer's eyes were close together and his gaze was penetrating. It seemed as if he was annoyed that Salim had interrupted him during a conversation.

"Salam Aleikum," he greeted back, but showed no trace of friendliness.

"This is the owner of the store," the salesman introduced Salim.

As if on cue, the customer's features suddenly brightened. He smiled slightly ingratiatingly and made a dismissive gesture with his hand. "Oh," he groaned, "I was just telling you about my bad luck. One of my horses was heavily pregnant and sick. The mare gave birth to a weak foal and died an hour after birth.

The newborn foal is weak, seems to have almost no sight, hardly eats, and is sickly. It's costing me money unnecessarily. Let's talk about something more pleasant.

37

He pointed to a few sacks of horse feed, three of which were for high performance sport horses. Next to the sacks were some bridles. "If I add two more bags, can you meet me on the price? Your salesman is a very tough negotiator. I'm glad you're here now."

Salim looked at the goods, made a quick calculation in his head and nodded. "If you let me take a look at the foal, I'll throw in a sack of sports feed for free."

The customer narrowed his eyes and seemed to do the same calculation. "If I double my purchase, will I get three extra sacks?"

Salim was smart and had expected something like this. He was very familiar with the business practices of the men who still practiced the old custom of haggling. As an experienced businessman, he knew that he would be successful if the customer thought he had made a good deal.

"If you double the amount, I'll throw in two bags of sports feed and one bag of mineral feed, and I'll deliver the goods to the farm free of charge. I would like to take a look at the foal there."

The customer's hand shot forward. It was as if he wanted to close the deal as quickly as possible before Salim could change his mind. "Agreed."

Hoping to take the foal with him and save it, Salim loaded the goods onto the horse trailer a short time later and drove off.

When he arrived at the customer's farm, they were already waiting for him. While one of the farm workers unloaded the feed, Salim and his client went into the stables.

There were some beautiful animals in the paddock. The farmer proudly spoke about the success of his animals. He led Salim along the paddock, past well-appointed stalls, to a small shed. Salim was startled to see the emaciated foal lying on the straw-covered floor under a shady tin roof.

"Here's this sick nag. I guess I can save the vet's fee to put it down. It won't survive the next week," the farmer said coldly.

Salim walked over to the foal and knelt down beside it. His emotions went on a merry-go-round. He alternated between pity for the animal and anger at the heartlessness of the man standing behind him. He stroked the foal's head, caressed its forehead, leaned forward and whispered a few words in its ear. Finally, his hands moved down the back to the sick foal's belly. He palpated, nodded wordlessly as if sensing something that could not be seen, and when he had finished his examination, the businessman stood up and said firmly, "I will buy the horse from you.

The owner looked astonished, narrowed his eyes again, and finally smiled thoughtfully. He seemed to be feverishly considering whether he had overlooked something about the foal. The horse breeder's head shook. Wrinkles formed on his forehead as he thought.

Was there really money to be made from the sick animal? Well, it was a purebred Berber. The loss of the mother was bitter. Even an inexpensive, moderately good mare costs about 9,000 euros on the European mainland, and the price is rising. That is the equivalent of about 100,000 Moroccan dirhams. As for the foal, the cost of euthanizing it would cost even more money. It was definitely too weak to survive, so he could rule out the possibility of it growing into a big, strong Berber mare.

He scratched his chin sheepishly and said to Salim: "You know the animal will die soon. Why do you want to buy it?"

"That is my business," Salim replied, trying to appear as cold and unemotional as possible.

The farmer's eyes wandered over the foal, scrutinizing it. "If we sign a contract, he won't give any money back," he hissed, as if he were a snake whose tongue spat out words.

Salim shook his hand. "I want to buy the colt and take the risk. I know it could die soon."

The farmer thought for a few seconds and murmured softly: "A healthy foal costs between 50,000 and 80,000 Moroccan dirhams."

Salim didn't think twice. He knew he had to act quickly if he wanted to help the horse. "I will pay 10,000 Moroccan dirhams. No more, no less. Put your money down or refuse. I'm leaving now," he bluffed, adding, "Either with or without ..." He pointed at the colt without finishing the sentence. There was not a trace of doubt in his voice. The sum Salim offered for the sick animal was a lot of money for a horse that would soon die and not much money for a Berber foal. At least if it grew up strong and healthy.

The farmer looked at Salim, glanced at his outstretched hand, looked at the foal, and then struck. "Ten thousand dirhams. Agreed. It's yours."

On his way back, Salim stopped to see a veterinarian friend who examined the foal in detail. He finally advised him to take the animal to the newly opened veterinary clinic, as it had the best equipment and "round-the-clock care".

Salim took the advice to heart and drove straight to the city. After taking care of everything, the animal lover returned home late that night. He told his family about the foal and received the psychological support he had hoped for. Again, the businessman had to pay a lot of money for the treatment. But Salim didn't care. What mattered to him was the welfare of the poor animal.

When he picked up the foal after two weeks at the clinic and brought it back to his farm, it was already looking better. It was standing up and hopping around, weak but clearly happy.

However, the veterinarian treating Salim had given him little hope. He thought the animal would only live for a few months. With a lot of luck, he thought, it might live a year or two at most. None of this mattered to Salim. He would take care of the foal and raise it with love.

"And if it is not given more time on this earth, it should enjoy its short life," he said, and his family agreed.

The foal was named Kala, which means sun. Salim was with Kala several times a day and the foal grew up. After only a year, it was impossible to tell that the Berber mare was a weak and seriously ill foal who was about to die. Kala and Salim were inseparable. It was as if an invisible bond held them together.

Contrary to all veterinary predictions, Kala lived to be two, then three, then four years old, and instead of dying, she grew stronger and more beautiful. By the time she was five, she was the real sunshine at Salim's farm and more than lived up to her name.

The Berber mare was playful, strong and majestic to look at. She followed Salim wherever he went, and the farmer and businessman often joked that Kala was his lapdog.

When asked about her condition at that time, Salim always replied: "I took such good care of Kala that she had no choice but to stay alive to become completely healthy and beautiful."

As fate would have it, Salim became so ill a few years later that he had to retire from business. His children took over the well-run business.

He was also no longer able to do the physically demanding work on the farm. The family hired a stable hand and Salim enjoyed his early retirement.

When Salim stopped going to the stables, Kala reversed the ritual. In the morning, before the sun had reached its full strength, the mare would trot from the stable to the house and wait for Salim. The two spent some time together before the horse trotted off to the paddock.

In the evening, as the hot sun set on the horizon, Salim would often sit on the veranda of his house. Even then, Kala would trot up, snort, and the two of them would end the day together.

When Salim was 65 years old, he collapsed one day in the garden behind his house. He was doing some light gardening when everything around him went black. He was not aware that he had hit the ground.

His wife found his lifeless body a short time later and immediately called for help. It was the weekend and the children were visiting. Salim's sons and daughter came running and carried their beloved father into the house. The shock was enormous. No one had expected anything so terrible. The doctor who was called finally confirmed what everyone had feared. He took his pulse and shook his head. "I'm afraid there's nothing I can do for him. He's gone."

The grief was great, the pain indescribable. Salim was a good and beloved man. He was respected by rich and poor, Muslims, Jews and Christians alike.

In keeping with the tradition of their region, the family immediately began making funeral arrangements. Salim was washed and wrapped in a shroud. Just one day later, he lay in a simple wooden coffin and was taken to the burial site, which was a short distance from the farm. Here were the graves of Salim's parents, grandparents, great-grandparents, and great-great-grandparents. Now his grave was dug.

Although it was a Christian funeral, there was a large crowd. In addition to family and distant relatives, there were many friends, business associates, and customers. Everyone wanted to pay their last respects to Salim.

When the funeral procession started to move and a priest wanted to give his eulogy at the grave, the groom had enormous problems keeping Kala calm. Contrary to her normal nature, the Berber mare was very impetuous. She resisted being taken to the stable and seemed to the farm worker like a wild horse.

After he managed to lock Kala in the stable, he hurried to the funeral procession. He didn't want to miss paying his last respects to his late employer. Behind him, he suddenly heard a muffled thud. Kala kicked at the wooden door with her hooves. The gate was old and somewhat dilapidated, but it still served its purpose. But Kala's strength was so great that after the fifth or sixth kick, the gate was torn from its anchors and fell out.

Kala took off. Snorting powerfully, he charged through the crowd of people, who jumped to their right and left to avoid being run over and seriously injured by the wild horse.

The wagon with the coffin stopped in front of the empty grave. The crowd had retreated a little. Everyone was staring at the horse, which seemed to have gone mad.

"We must shoot it!" shouted the crowd.

"Catch the animal!" someone else demanded.

"Tranquilize the horse!" was heard.

Murmurs and whispers finally drowned out the voices as Kala reached the coffin. The Berber mare stood and dropped her front hooves onto the lid of the coffin. Again and again, she slammed her hooves against the wood, splintering it bit by bit.

Anyone who knew Kala knew that the horse was anything but wild and dangerous. It was assumed that she missed her best friend and instinctively wanted to help him. But how do you tell an animal that a human has died?

"She needs to see the body," someone shouted.

The groom had reacted quickly and was running back to the stable to get a rope when Kala rushed up. He was now standing in front of the animal with it. He tied a noose and was about to throw it around the horse's neck.

With a loud crack, the coffin lid finally broke and stood wide open. Kala immediately stopped kicking and bent down. She sniffed into the coffin and whinnied loudly.

Silence fell. Shocked faces could be seen as a soft whimper came from the coffin. A few men immediately ran to the coffin. They couldn't believe what they saw.

"He's alive!" they heard.

"Father!"

The mourners surrounded the coffin in a mad rush to help. Tears of joy flowed.

"A doctor, quickly!"

"This is a miracle," prayed Salim's supposed widow.

Kala stood petrified the whole time. Finally, she let the rope be tied around her neck and followed the groom like a lamb as he led her away.

It was later determined that it was not a miracle and not magic. As incredible as Salim's story is, it can happen again and again.

What happened to Salim is known as an apparent death (Latin: vita reducta). Since Salim's body was also stiff, it was assumed that rigor mortis had set in. However, it was probably a case of catalepsy associated with suspended animation.

Simply put, it was a medical condition that mimicked death. It was a condition that was accompanied by complete loss of consciousness and even stiffness of the body. Such an event is very rare, but not impossible.

Thanks to the incredible bond between Kala and Salim, the horse sensed that its owner was still alive. By trampling on the coffin, he prevented Salim from being buried alive. This is a love that transcends our known boundaries.

Who would have thought that the weak and abandoned foal would one day save its rescuer from her own sad end?

The story of Salim and Kala is unique and shows how much an animal can love a human. Deep in their hearts, Salim and Kala remain forever connected.

There are many sayings and quotes about horses. One in particular applies to the story of Kala and Salim.

"Their hoofbeat is my heartbeat."

This is true love for horses and a bond between man and animal.

Dog Loyalty
in the Face of Death

True friends stick together. Even and especially in bad times. When someone is really sick and in danger, true friendship proves itself. Then it becomes clear how deep and stable this friendship really is. Do such friendships or bonds also exist in the animal world? Well, during my research I came across a story from the Ukraine that tells of a boundless friendship between two dogs.

Ukraine is one of the largest countries in Europe. Most of the country lies in the warm temperate zone. Especially the north and the northeast of the country are often influenced by the continental climate. This means harsh winters and warm summers. In the transitional periods, the so-called "Rasputiza" often prevails. This is the muddy period during the melting season. The soldiers of the various military invaders, such as Napoleon and his Grand Armée or Hitler's Wehrmacht in the Second World War, felt the effects of this.

Spring is generally considered the best time to visit Ukraine. By the end of April, the plants begin to bloom and the vast, fertile land is bathed in a colorful splendor of lush green.

You don't have to be a tourist to love this season. Vladimir Krushenko loved spring, too. Like almost every Saturday, the Ukrainian teacher set out early in the morning. Vladimir's equipment consisted of a few provisions, a tent, water and his camera. His routes took him through forests, farmland and swamps. He spent the night somewhere in the open and enjoyed the wilderness of the vast country. He enriched the classroom with his photographs, making subjects like geography and biology interesting. Some of his photos also made it into the daily newspaper or a magazine.

On this eventful day, his journey took him along the railroad tracks.

This non-electrified section of track was used primarily by freight trains. Heavy diesel locomotives pulled long wagons weighing tons.

Vladimir had already taken some good pictures and was satisfied with the day. He crossed the tracks and decided to follow them for two kilometers before turning into the forest. It was hot and he wanted to go through the forest down to the river. He wanted to swim there and make camp. He had found this place last summer. With a little luck, he might be able to lure a curious bear, get a few close-ups, and then scare it away with a loud air horn like the ones soccer fans use.

A good plan, he thought.

Vladimir was sweating. The air was getting warmer and he reached for his canteen. After a few hearty gulps, he wanted to keep going, but he recognized something on the tracks and stopped. Something was in the middle of the track bed and wasn't moving. The teacher couldn't make out what it was. He thought it was an animal carcass and walked curiously toward his discovery.

It could be a hiker who has fallen and needs help, he thought next. Excited, he accelerated a bit and then stopped abruptly. This something lying in the middle of the track bed had moved.

"It's definitely not human," he muttered. "And certainly not a dead animal!"

The teacher suspected that he was needed. Something seemed to be stuck, and the next freight train could arrive at any moment.

Seeing this danger, Vladimir began to run and quickly approached. He noticed that there were two dogs. Both were lying in the middle of the track bed.

"Get away!" he shouted, gradually slowing his run until he was back to a normal walking pace. He was panting. Dark patches of sweat formed under his shirt, and thick beads of sweat ran down his forehead and cheeks.

Everyone knows the sound of an approaching train. At first it is barely audible, then that heavy, dull hum grows and suddenly it rushes past you with an insane force. You feel the pull and the power of the many tons of weight.

And it was this low but powerful humming that Vladimir heard at that moment. A freight train would pass here in an instant and crush everything on the tracks. Two dogs were no obstacle to thousands of tons of steel.

The teacher was aware of the pull of a passing train and kept his distance from the tracks.

"Get away!" he shouted in panic at the two dogs, but they didn't listen. He immediately pulled out his red scarf and began waving it wildly to get the driver's attention and make him brake hard. Vladimir waved his arms and the scarf wildly. He waved it as if his own life was at stake. He shouted at the top of his lungs: "Stop! Stop!" even though he knew the engineer couldn't hear him.

It came as it had to. Vladimir's stop signals were not seen, and if they were, they were ignored. Although the freight train was traveling much slower than a modern passenger train due to the tons of cargo, it maintained its speed undiminished.

The Teacher closed his eyes. He couldn't bear the sight of the locomotive hitting and killing the two dogs. His whole body shook as the freight train passed him by.

Ch...damm damm ... ch...damm damm

He had to endure this noise for almost minutes until the last car finally passed. A thick lump had formed in Vladimir's throat. He could hardly swallow. He knew he had a sad task ahead of him. He had to collect the carcasses of the dead animals and bury them. Hopefully the image wasn't too gruesome. Tears welled up in the animal lover's eyes.

Ch...damm damm ... ch...damm damm

The heavily loaded wagons of the long freight train rumbled incessantly past him. Thoughts raced through the teacher's mind.

If the dogs wear a collar with a reference to the owner, I'll go to him, he decided. The last car rushed by. The further away the train went, the quieter it became.

Vladimir looked ahead. The teacher thought he saw a mirage. The sun was high and it was wonderfully warm, but there was no shimmering heat. It must be an illusion. He must have been mistaken. Perhaps a last breeze from the heavily loaded wagons?

"No!" Vladimir shouted, certain that the dogs were alive. "A miracle," he pressed his lips together, barely audible.

The two dogs in the track bed moved. One was lying on the sleepers with its head raised, the other had gotten up and was standing. It lifted its snout slightly and sniffed in Vladimir's direction. They were mongrels. As the train passed over them, they lay down flat and stayed there until the entire freight train had passed over them. Apparently they both survived unharmed. When the teacher was only a few feet away from the dogs, the standing dog walked up to him, lifted his lips and growled. He made it clear to Vladimir that this was the end of the line.

Grrrrr ...

"It's all right," the teacher whispered in a soothing voice. He stopped and took another step back with another growl. "I'm your friend. What's going on?" Vladimir spoke in a low voice, as if the dog could understand him.

After taking two more steps back, the dog turned and went back to the second dog. Now Vladimir realized that the second dog was injured. He didn't seem to be able to move and obviously couldn't get up to leave the track bed.

"For God's sake," he exclaimed. What fear these two dogs must have suffered as the long freight train rolled over them? And it might not even have been the first train. How long had this been going on? Those poor animals.

The teacher admired the loyalty of the healthy animal. It stayed with its friend and protected him. Even in the mortal danger of an approaching train, it never left the side of its injured comrade.

Vladimir knew that he couldn't approach without being bitten. He pulled out his cell phone. A hopeful look at the display. He had reception. He quickly punched in an emergency number and tried to describe the situation as best he could.

It took more than an hour for a small rescue team to arrive on the scene. It consisted of a veterinarian and an assistant. The injured dog was caught using a pole with a noose and locked in a dog crate. The injured dog was less aggressive. Maybe it was just too weak.

"A fracture. It's very likely that the dog was hit by a train. I've injected him with a painkiller and brought the animals to my office," explained Vladimir the vet. "I'll operate today."

"Thank you."

"Are these your dogs?" the helper wanted to know and wrote down Vladimir's name and address.

"No," he shook his head. "I just found them."

She smiled. "Lucky for the animals."

The vet closed the tailgate of his SUV. "A loyal dog. He protected his friend! That's true love," he grinned.

Barely a minute later, the next freight train rolled past the rescue team. Full of respect and aware of how dangerous the healthy dog's actions were, they looked at the speeding cars.

Ch...damm damm ... ch...damm damm

Vladimir pointed at the vet's car. "You operate without knowing if you'll be reimbursed?"

An approving nod. "This is a young dog with a few good years of life ahead of him. I became a veterinarian to help animals. If I'm stuck with the costs, that's the way it is."

The teacher pondered, scratched the back of his head, and said: "I have an idea. Could you stand next to the tracks? I'd like to take a picture."

The next day, a large article appeared in the local section of the daily newspaper. It was about animal love, loyalty, courage, and a veterinarian with a big heart for animals.

At the end of the article, people were asked to provide information about the owners. There was also an appeal for donations to help pay for the surgery.

A few days later, the owners were found. They were from the neighboring district. Acquaintances had read the story in the newspaper and called the owner.

The dogs had stumbled across a deer trail while out for a walk and had run away. Despite an intensive search, they were not found. When they did not return home the next day, he put out search notices in the area, but they were not very successful.

After receiving a tip from his friend, he immediately drove to the veterinarian's office. The elderly gentleman was greeted with great joy by his dogs. He was happy to pay for the surgery and also put something in the donation box. "This is for all the animals you treat and don't get paid for," he said as he left.

This mixed-breed dog from Ukraine proved the power of loyalty and love. Even though his life was in danger, he never left his injured friend.

The male dog never left the injured female dog alone on the tracks for a second, even though he was very scared himself. That's what I call true friendship.

Jikitaya, the Jaguar

The Amazon is the longest river in the world with a length of 6788 kilometers and is also the main river of the largest river system on our planet. It is fed by more than 10,000 tributaries, some of which are over 1600 kilometers long.

At its mouth, the river is over 300 Km wide. Inland, the Amazon is about 20 km wide during the dry season and up to 48 km wide at high tide.

Even the tides affect the Amazon and can be felt up to 700 kilometers inland.

At full moon and new moon, waves of water up to five meters high roll up the river. The Indians who live along the river's banks respectfully call this phenomenon pororocá, or thundering water.

Amazonia, as the area of the giant river is called, is one of the richest regions in the world in terms of flora and fauna. The impressive beauty of nature captivates every visitor. Unfortunately, the abundance of natural resources and tropical timber also has its drawbacks. Gold prospectors and the timber industry not only destroy the unique natural environment, but also displace the indigenous people and many animal species. The land will be destroyed for decades, if not centuries, as a result of this over-exploitation of nature.

A large part of Amazonia belongs to Brazil. In order to stop this criminal activity, the Brazilian government has begun to send soldiers into the Amazon region. The brave men and women of the Brazilian Army have been roaming the rainforest region for several years. They protect the land, the people and the animals. They confront criminal gold-diggers, stop illegal logging, and even fight fires when large swaths of forest are set ablaze by unauthorized slash-and-burn.

One such soldier was Gabriel Alves. *(*Author's note: the names of the characters are fictitious - any similarities to the real names of the jaguar rescuers would be coincidental)*

59

The young man has come a long way in his life. Gabriel comes from the favelas of Rio de Janeiro, and no one around him ever believed he could break out of the slums. He followed his dream, went to school and eventually became a soldier. In the army, he quickly worked his way up to the rank of sergeant. He was a sergeant in the Brazilian Army, a terceiro-sargento.

As a child of a favela, Gabriel knew exactly what it meant to overcome difficult situations, and he also knew that there are particularly difficult situations in life that you can't overcome without outside help, and in the worst case, you won't survive.

He was proud of his country, proud of its beauty, and proud to serve as a soldier to protect it.

It was sweltering hot that day. Sergeant Gabriel Alves was leading his squad through the Brazilian rainforest. A radio call had come in from headquarters that there were some gold miners in their patrol area. Indians had spotted them and reported the incident. Allegedly, the men were traveling by boat and had continued upstream. Sergeant Alves was ordered to find the natives, question them, and follow the prospectors' trail. Illegal gold miners are destroying nature through radical digging, destroying valuable habitat for animals and the indigenous people who live there.

"The mosquitoes are aggressive today," cursed Maria Da Silva, slapping her face with the flat of her hand and looking at her prey. The soldier walked a few steps behind Gabriel and brushed the dead mosquito from her uniform pants.

Wordlessly, Gabriel reached into his left breast pocket and pulled out a small spray. "Here," he said, handing it to Maria. "Spray yourself with it. Smells like hell, but the mosquitoes don't like it."

After a few pumps, she handed the mosquito repellent back. "Thanks, Gabriel. Even if the stuff works, we have to be back by dusk or the big swarms of mosquitoes will come and eat us," she grumbled.

Gabriel laughed. "This is the jungle."

Corporal Luiz Sosa asked from behind: "How much further is it? The Pororocá seems to have passed. If the big wave is gone, the prospectors must be gone too. I guess they were just looking for shelter from the tidal wave on the shore."

Gabriel raised his hand to signal him to stop. He wiped drops of sweat from his forehead with the sleeve of his uniform. Then the sergeant pulled a map from the side pocket of his trousers, flipped it open and ran his right index finger over it. He found what he was looking for, and the finger pointed to a specific spot.

A few monkeys crouched in the dense green of the trees, watching the uniformed group. Birds made various sounds and something scurried through the undergrowth.

"Another two hundred meters and we're on the shore, right where the natives told us to be.

Maria took a drink of water. If Gabriel said they were right, then they were right. The sergeant seemed to have grown up with the jungle, even though he hadn't grown up here, but in Rio de Janeiro.

"Not a sound from now on. Get the weapons ready. If they're still there, I want to surprise them."

The guns were checked and the safety released in case of emergency. Everyone in the group was ready to defend themselves and cover the person in front of them or next to them if the prospectors offered armed resistance.

Gabriel waited until everyone was finished, then gave another hand signal. Wordlessly, the group moved toward the shore. Trying to move as quietly as possible, they approached the presumed camp site.

As the Amazon appeared in front of them, the sight was mesmerizing. The world's most famous river flowed before them toward the ocean. The mighty river was in flood.

It was just as Corporal Sosa had suspected. The great wave had long since thundered past, but it had brought enormous masses of water with it. There was nothing left of the prospectors except an abandoned campsite and two empty cans.

Sosa knelt before a burned-out campfire and reached into the ashes. "Cold. They've been gone a while."

Maria looked at the river. "If they left right after the wave, they've got quite a head start."

Gabriel took notes.

Maria paused. "There's something!" Her outstretched hand pointed to the water.

The entire group of soldiers immediately lined up on the shore. They watched in horror as a young jaguar struggled for its life in the floodwaters.

"We have to do something?" Maria cried shrilly. Her voice cracked. She looked to Gabriel for help.

"Now it's sunk," Luiz Sosa roared.

Maria cupped her hands over her eyes. "Oh my God, it's such a young animal. How terrible! We have to do something," she repeated.

"It's coming up again!" a young soldier shouted excitedly, pointing at the swimming jaguar.

63

Gabriel Alves knew that the big cat had been on the Washington Convention's list of endangered species since the 1970s. The sergeant noticed that the young animal's strength was dwindling. The great tidal wave must have swept the jaguar away. The big cat's head kept diving under the water. It was in danger of drowning, and with an iron will to survive, it managed to lift its head above the surface again and again. Air was being sucked in.

Gabriel reacted. He could no longer stand by and watch the scene unfold. He threw his rifle aside and opened the paddock, took off his boots, pants, and uniform jacket, and bravely jumped into the water.

"Help him! Form a chain so the sergeant doesn't drift away!" demanded Corporal Sosa, who also slipped out of his uniform. Maria stomped into the water immediately. She didn't care if her uniform got wet. Three other soldiers immediately followed. The group formed a human chain. They held hands for safety. The soldier at the front was also the tallest. The river water was up to his chest.

Gabriel swam against the current with strong strokes and approached the young jaguar.

"Come on, you can do it!" he was cheered.

"Sergeant, Sergeant!" came from some of the men in repeated chants.

Gabriel could feel the power of the water. "Hang on!" he gasped to the drowning animal. Thoughts flashed through his mind. Would the wild beast resist rescue? Would it see him as a threat and bite? Would the feline predator run its sharp claws through his face and hurt him? Might he lose an eye?

The soldier swallowed water and spat it out with a cough. He dismissed the thoughts as quickly as they had come and pulled his arms through the waves of the Amazon even harder than before.

As if the young jaguar recognized the rescue attempt, he gave his last strength and tried to swim towards the human, his only enemy in the entire Amazon region.

"Sergeant... Sergeant!" his group urged him on.

Alves felt himself fading, gritted his teeth and swam on.

Three more meters, two more. In a few moments, two different creatures that would have considered each other enemies in the wild would meet.

The moment when Sergeant Gabriel Alves reached for the jaguar was indescribable for him. He grabbed the exhausted animal by the neck like a cat, at the exact moment when it had probably lost its last strength and was sinking. With a strong tug, he lifted the jaguar's head above the water, turned it onto its back and laid its head on his chest. The jaguar stopped moving and let everything happen. The big cat's eyes stared at its rescuer as he tried to swim backward to shore.

Gabriel had great respect for the animal. Jaguars have long, dangerous canines and the strongest teeth of any big cat. Their bite is twice as powerful as a lion's. But this young animal was

65

anything but dangerous at this moment. It lay calmly on the soldier's chest and let itself be dragged through the water.

Two soldiers swam to their sergeant and helped him swim back until they reached the small human chain and the strong arm of the big soldier took hold. On the shore, Gabriel set the jaguar down and sat down beside it, exhausted. He was panting. His chest rose and fell with each breath.

"You're a hero," Maria cheered, daring to stroke the animal's back with the flat of her hand.

"What do we do with him?" asked Corporal Sosa.

Silence.

Everyone stared at the weakened animal lying motionless on the bank. His breathing was shallow but steady.

"If we don't take him with us, he'll either be killed by a rival or worse, found by poachers." Maria crossed her arms to look even more energetic.

Sergeant Alves slipped into his dry uniform. He had already made a decision. "Radio operator," he called to the man with the radio. "Contact the base. The message is: the Indians have been questioned, we've tracked the poachers to the Amazon. They're gone, probably upstream. Our task force was able to save a young jaguar from drowning and pull it out of the water. The animal is helpless. We ask you to contact and inform the local authorities and take the jaguar with you! We will return. End of radio message." The group packed up. The weak animal was placed on a stretcher, which was carried as an emergency stretcher for any casualties. Members of the small military unit took turns carrying the animal.

Once at the base, the jaguar was taken to a veterinarian. After examinations, the authorities made the unique decision weeks later to allow the wild jaguar to stay with the Brazilian Army and Sergeant Alves' group.

One reason for this decision was that the jaguar had long since become accustomed to its rescuers and had made friends with them. Releasing it back into the wild was no longer an option.

The big cat was named Jikitaya and became the troupe's mascot. Jikitaya played with his new family and accompanied them like a dog. He even wore a collar and walked on a leash.

Jikitaya is still living with his rescuers. Their care and love has turned him into a tame predator.

The soldiers helped the most dangerous hunter in the Amazon region by bravely diving into the waters of the Amazon to pull him out of the water.
A precious life was saved. The life of a jaguar.

Sergeant Gabriel Alves had done a great service not only to his country, but also to wildlife.

A wolf called "Ear

It has long been debated whether and for how long dogs and wolves can remember experiences or encounters. While some studies have suggested that dogs and wolves forget events within two minutes, more recent studies have shown that these four-legged friends have episodic and declarative memory. This means that they can recall past experiences and encounters.

This is even more pronounced in wolves than in dogs. When a dog changes owners, it usually forgets the previous owner sometime within the next three years. However, events or recurring smells from this period trigger a kind of recognition.

In short, dogs never forget a person who has done something good to them or a person who has done something bad to them. Simply put, this thought information is stored in their brains and can trigger a memory through an experience or a certain smell.

The story of the wolf named Ear is one such experience.

Medical students Mark and Mary-Ann met and fell in love in college. They became a couple, successfully completed their studies, and gained their first practical experience in a clinic.

They never lost sight of their goal: they had decided to move to the countryside together, partly to set an example against the rural exodus that was massively moving to the cities, and partly to pursue their hobbies. Hunting and nature photography. As hunters, they occasionally shot some waterfowl or a deer, but only when the animal population grew too much and became harmful to nature. Most of the time, the camera was their weapon.

Both loved wildlife photography more than anything else. Voyageurs National Park offered the best conditions for their hobby. The young doctors found a well-paying job at a hospital and bought a house in the rural area. They also set up a small practice there, which they ran in addition to their hospital work for the villagers.

Whenever they had time, they hiked through the national park. Mary-Ann and Mark had done it. They were living their dream.

Ear's story began on a glorious fall day. The sun had made another effort and was casting its warm rays over Voyageurs National Park in Minnesota. Mary-Ann and Mark were out with their cameras again.

"Who needs the East Coast's famous Indian summer?" the young doctor exclaimed, pointing to the center of the canopy. "We have a blaze of color here that can easily compete with New England's."

Mary-Ann laughed. "You could write a guidebook to Minnesota right now."

The leaves rustled with each step they took. They both knew that with the noise they were making, they were guaranteed not to get any deer on camera. They didn't care. They had had a wonderful day and had enjoyed a long picnic in a clearing at noon. Now they were heading back to their car.

"Did you switch shifts with Dr. Lynn tomorrow?" asked Mark.

Mary-Ann nodded. "Yes, her mother is turning 75 and she wants to surprise her and drive her home to celebrate."

"To New York?"

"Yes," Mary-Ann confirmed, "and Dr. Lynn is taking over Friday of next week. That means I can take her bowling."

"Great!" Mark was pleased and stopped. He thought he heard something. "Wait a minute," he said, listening. "There was something. Did you hear it?"

Mary-Ann stopped. They were both silent. Except for the chirping of a few birds, there was nothing to be heard. Mary-Ann shook her head. "No. There's nothing."

Mark raised his hand as if to signal a halt. "I'm sure there was something. It sounded like a beeping."

Both remained silent. Silence. Mary-Ann was about to wave goodbye, saying that Mark must have been imagining things, when she heard a faint beeping, too. "Now I hear it too."

They both tried to find the direction. Finally, Mark pointed to the right and started walking. Mary-Ann followed him. They kept stopping, listening, trying to locate the sound. After a few minutes, they were able to locate it. Shortly after, they spotted a wolf cub.

The animal lifted its head feebly. It lay in a small pool of blood, and part of its right ear was missing.

"For God's sake," the doctor groaned. "Mark, we have to help the poor thing."

Without looking at his wife, Mark knelt down.

"Be careful, he might snap at you. Wolves are usually very shy."

Ignoring the warning, he stroked the wolf's fur. There was no attempt to catch it. The wounded animal lay motionless. In fact, it seemed to enjoy being stroked. Like a child seeking its mother's comforting hand when it has been hurt. "He's so weak."

Both looked around to see if the mother, or even the entire pack, was looking for her cubs.

"Female wolves usually give birth in April or May. So the little male would be about three or four months old," Mary-Ann estimated.

Mark nodded. "The age would be consistent with the size."

They suspected the cause of the serious injury was a fight. The young wolf had apparently been separated from its pack and then encountered an animal that had chased and injured it. The medical couple did not hesitate for a second in deciding to help the wolf. They carefully placed the injured animal on their picnic blanket and carried it to the car.

When they arrived home, they immediately brought the weakened wolf into their office. They cleaned, disinfected, and sutured the wounds. After treatment, they laid the animal on Mark's old blanket.

"He's soft here and he'll get used to your smell," was Mary-Ann's comment.

While Mark sat with the wolf, his wife went back into town to buy dog food. She chose a nutritious puppy food and hoped the young wolf would regain his strength quickly.

Later, Mark and Mary-Ann took turns keeping watch during the night. During the night watch, they came up with the idea of naming the wolf Ear because of the half severed ear.

The young wolf slept a lot. Whenever he woke up, he would lift his head briefly and sniff at Mark and Mary-Ann's hands. He accepted the first morsels of food from Mark's hands, which he carefully pushed into his mouth with his tongue. As soon as Ear was able to sit up on his own, they stopped feeding him by hand. They didn't want him to get used to people.

The previous owner of the house had kept several dogs in a large kennel. Mark was glad he hadn't torn it down yet. The big kennel was the perfect home for Ear. The next morning, they took the wolf into the kennel and placed food and fresh water inside.

Ear recovered surprisingly quickly, but seemed anything but happy. He spent most of his time lying in one of the three dog kennels, leaving it only to eat or drink.

Mark let Ear sniff his hand and sleeve whenever he brought food or checked his wounds.

The wolf hid during the day and howled at night. Sometimes a response would come from the nearby national park, and individual wolf howls would swell into a concert.

Once Ear was fully recovered, Mark and Mary-Ann knew they had to release the wolf. He was and would remain a wild animal. They waited for the right time and, with heavy hearts, opened the kennel when Ear again joined in a wolf howl. The decision had not been easy for them, as they had both grown to love the young wolf.

When the kennel door was wide open, they took a few steps to the side. "Out with you, old friend. They're calling you," Mark said.

As if Ear had understood the words, he stuck his snout out of the open kennel. He lifted his nose to the wind and sniffed. Slowly, very carefully, he left his little shelter. Paw by paw, he was picked up and carefully placed on the ground. It was as if the wolf was stalking his prey. Finally, he ran off and chased across the large meadow toward the forest. The doctor and his wife embraced. "He's free again, and he loves his freedom."

"You said it, Mark. He's happy now. I just hope he goes his way."

The couple left the kennel open for two weeks. They secretly hoped that Ear would come back and greet them like a dog, but Ear was a wild animal. He was a wolf whose home was the National Park. That was where he belonged. That was where his pack lived. In short, Ear didn't come back.

The experience with the young wolf was very present in the beginning. Mark and Mary-Ann told their friends and colleagues about the injured animal and how they nursed it back to health. Hunting and hiking friends even kept an eye out for Ear on their trips. They hoped to spot him and tell the couple, but the national park was huge and wolves roamed far and wide. With its pristine national parks, the vast north-central U.S. provides important retreats for the endangered animals.

After a few weeks and months the meeting was slowly forgotten. A few photos still reminded me of Ear, but after three years they were just part of a huge collection of beautiful wildlife photos.

Minnesota is famous for its harsh winters. Cold polar winds keep the state, located in the north of the USA and bordering Canada, in a frosty grip.

Mark and Mary-Ann also loved the cold side of their home. Just as they roamed the state in spring, summer, and fall, they also set out in winter.

Equipped with snowshoes, thermos flasks, and cameras, they roamed the national park to take beautiful winter photographs. They also hunted deer from time to time. Especially when there was too much browsing on the young trees and the animals became pests.

Mark had bought new snowshoes and was eager to try them out. The weather forecast was good on this cold winter's day. The sun was shining and millions of tiny ice crystals shone like tiny mirrors on the white blanket of snow.

"I'll be back before dark," he said goodbye to Mary-Ann.

He zipped up his parka, put on his sunglasses, and trudged off. A haze of breath wafted in front of his face, and snow crunched under his every step. Soon he had disappeared into the forest. Mark had chosen one of his favorite routes off the main trail. He felt a sense of freedom and adventure.

"This must have been how the old trappers felt 200 years ago," it flashed through his mind. "Alone in the wilderness."

Mark was more than happy with his new snowshoes. He was going to have a lot of fun with them. They were light yet sturdy. He literally glided over the snow.

Mark had long since passed the wide clearing and was on his way back when he saw a trail of blood. Large paws had been pressed into the thin layer of ice that had formed on the snow.

"A lynx must have killed a deer," he realized and followed the trail curiously. Maybe he could get a good picture. With luck, he even caught the bobcat eating.

The trail ended in front of a tree. The big cat had hidden the carcass there and covered it with snow.

"Just one picture, then I'm going home," Mark decided, slowly approaching the hidden prey. There was no sign of the lynx for miles around. No doubt it had eaten long ago and was circling its territory.

The doctor stomped off. A loud click was heard.

Snap

At the same time a sharp pain shot through Mark's right leg. He fell to the snow with a loud scream.

"Ahhh!"

He realized immediately what had happened. The straps of a plate trap were around his right ankle, holding him down with great pressure.

The pain was indescribable. The force of the catch had broken the bone and pinned his foot. The doctor was on the verge of fainting. Every movement sent an almost unbearable wave of pain through his body.

"Stay conscious!" he said to himself, lying still for a moment and breathing calmly. He gathered his strength and thought of a solution to his problem.

He and his wife hated this kind of traps. They were pure torture for all animals. They were not allowed to use this type of trap in this area. Besides, hunting was strictly forbidden here anyway!

"They were poachers. Miserable bastards," grumbled the injured man.

Mark pushed the thoughts out of his head. He had to concentrate on a solution and analyzed his situation. The doctor was out of town and it was winter. The dead deer would surely attract other carnivores as well as the bobcat. And in the worst case, wolves. That was a danger. If the smell of the carcass didn't attract any animals, there was another deadly danger hovering over him. With the onset of darkness, the temperature would drop even further, well below freezing point. He was in danger of freezing to death. The pain in his leg was indescribable. The doctor determined that it was broken. With luck, a clean break.

He closed his eyes for a moment and opened them again. Time had become the most important factor. It was at least five miles to the house, more like seven or eight. A long distance to cover with a broken leg. Mark tried to ignore the pain and concentrate on finding a solution. There weren't many options left, so he made a decision. He would try to go home despite the painful injury.

"Now!" he said loudly and sat up. The situation was catastrophic. A look at his lower leg confirmed his worst suspicions. The trap had shattered the bone. The wound was bleeding slightly. Fortunately, Mark was athletic and not overweight. He leaned forward and bent the trap back. Again, this almost unbearable pain seized all his nerves. It felt like someone was hammering his lower leg.

Mark was overcome with rage as he took a closer look at the leghold trap. How much the trapped animals had to suffer. He had heard of wolves biting off their own legs to free themselves from such a cruel trap in order to survive.

The more anger he felt, the more determined Mark became. He grabbed the safety latches and bent them back to their original position. The resistance was less than he had feared. He held the stirrups apart and lifted the broken leg. Stars danced before his eyes as he endured several waves of pain in succession. He set the broken foot down in the snow. He let the shackle snap shut so it would not serve its cruel purpose a second time.

After a short rest, Mark tried to get up, but gave up while he was still trying. There was no way he could put any weight on his broken leg. It was an impossibility.

"Damn it!" he cursed.

It would be dark soon. He had the choice of spending the night here or crawling home. The wound could get infected. For a moment he considered building an emergency shelter out of snow. He and Mary-Ann had taken a survival course two years ago. The more he thought about it, the faster he dismissed the idea. Trying to crawl home was more promising. He would keep moving, and movement meant warmth, and warmth meant not freezing to death. He also wanted to get to a hospital as soon as possible.

"Time is my opponent and I will win this duel," he said aloud to himself to encourage himself.

Mark crawled away. The pain was there, but it was much more bearable than trying to stand up.

"The crawling works. I can do it," he said, encouraging himself.

Foot by foot, the doctor crawled across the white blanket of snow. Beads of sweat quickly formed on his forehead. A few strands of blond hair stuck out from under his warm woolen hat. They stuck to his skin, soaked with sweat. He had to at least reach the wide trail. If he didn't make it home for some reason, they would find him on the way. The first search party would certainly go that way. He was absolutely sure of it.

Mark used the two snowshoes as a kind of glove and crawling aid. He grabbed the front strap. His forearms rested on the flat board. This allowed him to support himself halfway and keep his hands from sinking into the snow. He used his good leg to support the forward thrust, pulling the broken one along as motionlessly as possible. It would take him a long time to cover the distance. That was clear, and he wondered when Mary-Ann would start to worry about him.

Would it be at nightfall or some time later, when it was already dark? Will she try it alone and come to me? Or would she call the sheriff to organize a search party?

Lost in these thoughts, he walked the first five or six hundred meters. The forest was quiet. Except for the cracking of the thin layer of ice on the snowbed, there was hardly any sound to be heard. It was reassuring on one hand, but on the other, the silence frightened him. Mark paused for a moment and stopped. He looked around and saw the wide track in the snow. The howling of a wolf made him jump. When other animals of the pack joined in, he became afraid. He feared that a pack had gathered to hunt and might come across his track.

Whooooooo

The volume of the howling sent a shiver down his spine. The pack was close, he was sure of it. What could he do?

Panic struck him. Mark continued to struggle through the snow. He was panting, sweating, and driven by the will to survive. Soon the first mile was done. The doctor got his bearings and headed in the right direction toward the wide trail. He realized with trepidation that dawn was breaking.

"Damn it!"

He should have turned back sooner. Sounds made him sit up and listen. Was that panting?

It happened within seconds. A wolf appeared a few meters in front of him. Startled, the doctor stayed where he was. He turned on his back and sat up. Within seconds he was surrounded by several wolves. They were cautious, perhaps suspicious, because the human was their enemy. They probably saw him as easy prey. One of the wolves parted its lips. A growl could be heard. Goose bumps ran down Mark's spine. If only he had brought his rifle or revolver. A warning shot might have scared the wolves away. He was shaking, scared to death.

"Get away!" he shouted loudly, but instead of fleeing, the circle of animals grew closer around him.

Mark patted the snow with his snowshoes. "Get out of here! Help!"

The call went unheard. It was as if the forest swallowed the calls and did not carry them any further. The wolves were about to attack him. He would lose his life here and now. Mark stared at the wolf standing directly in front of him, its teeth bared.

Still five meters away, he estimated. It's about to attack.

A strong male came running up from the side, crossed the path of the animal in front of him and pushed him back, growling. The wolf then turned and circled Mark once at a safe distance. When it was behind Mark's back, it approached him very slowly and very carefully. The sniffing could be heard.

Meanwhile, the other wolves stayed where they were, as if on command.

"It must be the lead wolf," Mark thought, his back still covered in goose bumps.

Only the leader could keep the hungry pack at bay. The strong animal held its nose to the wind and sniffed as it approached very cautiously. Finally, the wolf went into a kind of crouch, stretching his head far forward so that he could pull his whole body back in a flash if danger came.

Two more wolves scurried up, but were immediately sent back with a growl and a light snap from the lead wolf. The big wolf was now at Mark's side. The doctor dared not turn his head. As the wolf got closer and the wet nose was only six inches from Mark's head, the doctor's whole body shook. He was terrified and didn't dare move an inch.

The wolf took another step and was now standing directly across from Mark. The injured doctor looked at the powerful animal. Warm breath rushed towards him. Yellow eyes focused on him. Mark's eyes moved up along the head and he couldn't believe what he saw. A large part of the dog's right ear was missing.

"Ear?" Mark whispered very quietly so as not to startle the wolf. "Ear, is that you?" came a little louder, but still in a low voice.

He thought he heard some kind of tail wagging. "Ear, my friend, do you recognize me? I rescued you a long time ago."

Talking did him good. It took away the fear, if only for a few moments. It helped him get over the moment of the dreaded attack and gave him hope. Hope that the big wolf standing in front of him was his Ear. Ear, the wolf whose life he had saved years ago.

Could it really be so? Could a young wolf, running alone back into the wild, grow up unharmed, survive and form his own pack?

"Ear. That's your name. That's what we used to call you."

While Mark was still talking to the wolf, it turned away from him and made a lap around the supposed human prey. No

85

member of the pack dared attack Mark. Ear motioned to his pack to retreat. One by one, the animals retreated. Ear came back to Mark. He padded cautiously up and sniffed the injured doctor again. He brushed his tongue across Mark's cheek once, and then Ear sat down beside Mark.

A wolf howled in the distance. Loud growls could be heard. The pack must have discovered the deer carcass. Ear lifted his head and, wrapped in a haze of warm lung air, let out a long howl from his throat.

Mark was relieved. He slowly lost the tension of the expected death and felt protected. The wolf had recognized him. It was a small miracle.

"What are we going to do now?" he asked Ear, who was staring at him with a slight tilt of his head. "You'll take care of me? That's a really good move on your part."

The doctor knew he had to keep crawling. His strength was fading and he thought his body temperature was rising. Fever! He had to move on if he wanted to survive. Now!

"Ear, don't get scared, but I have to go," he whispered and lay down on his stomach again. Mark took a deep breath and started to crawl again.

Ear waited a moment. Then the wolf stood up and walked very slowly next to Mark. He accompanied him. Ear was unmistakably protecting the man who had saved his life years ago. The wolf did not leave the injured man's side. When Mark took a rest and lay down, Ear came closer and sniffed him.

"It's all right, my friend. I'm still alive. I just need to rest a little," he said to the animal, and Ear sat down and waited.

Mark felt protected. Ear's presence gave him strength. So much strength that he managed to crawl out to the wide path. It was dark now and Mark was panting, sweating and at the end of his tether. His arms hurt almost as much as his broken leg. If he collapsed now, Ear would definitely lie down next to him and try to keep him warm. The wolf repaid his debt by showing friendship and loyalty that no one had thought possible. But Mark also knew that Ear was a wild wolf and had to get back to his pack. He wouldn't stay forever and would eventually disappear into the woods as he had before.

Ear heard the search party long before Mark could see even a small glimmer of light from the flashlights. The wolf stood up and looked at Mark. The doctor would have liked to pet him, but his arms were too weak to lift. The eyes of the wolf and the human met one last time. Finally, Ear raised his head, let out a long howl, turned and disappeared into the forest.

Mark remained seated, watching his faithful friend. He could no longer see him and stared into the darkness. He instinctively felt that Ear was somewhere in the forest, watching him.

Mary-Ann and a couple of men arrived shouting "Mark". Their flashlight light traveled across the trail and between the snow-covered trees.

When the first cone of light grazed the doctor and someone shouted, "There he is!" Mark knew that Ear was now running back to his pack, satisfied.

"Mark!" cried Mary-Ann, "I was so frightened for you when we heard the wolves howling.

"That was Ear," the doctor replied, trying to smile.

Mark was rushed to the hospital and operated on. After his leg healed, he often went to the national park. He never saw Ear again, but he will never forget the wolf. Just as the wolf will never forget him.

And sometimes, when he hears the wolves howling, Mark thinks that Ear is calling out to him to make sure he is okay.

Mansur the Bear

Can people and animals become friends?

The answer to that question is a resounding yes! Countless stories tell of it, and cats and dogs live in millions of homes. The latter were already known as man's best friend.

But there are not only friendships between domesticated animals and humans, but also between humans and wild animals. The following story is an example of this. It shows that animals can develop feelings not only for other animals, but also for humans. And it shows how important loyalty and care can be and how they can be rewarded.

The small Orlovka airfield in the Tver Oblast is located about 170 kilometers northwest of Moscow in central Russia. There is one runway, one hangar, and a lot of greenery. Half of Tver Oblast is forested. Life in the countryside is quiet, and when the pilots at the small airfield are not teaching a few lessons or taking off for a sightseeing flight or a parachute jump, they are tinkering with one of the five historic aircraft parked there.

One of the pilots is Andrei Ivanov. Andrei loves to fly, and when there are no customers around, he is either sitting in the cockpit of the old passenger plane, repairing the instrument displays, or crawling around somewhere in the workshop under one of the aircraft engines with oil-smeared hands. He has found his happiness here on earth. Andrey loves flying, airplanes and his colleagues.

On that day in April 2016 it was business as usual. There was no flight order, so Andrey and his colleague Yuri were in the workshop working on an engine. It was very warm for April and the hangar door was wide open. The two pilots were chatting animatedly about the upcoming European Soccer Championship.

"So tell me, Andrei, are you related to midfielder Oleg Ivanov or not?"

This question had been discussed among the pilots for weeks. Andrei allowed himself a joke now and then, promising to get tickets and auction them off to the highest bidder.

Andrei laughed. "Ha, ha. You just don't let up, Yuri. Just think about it. Where did I come from?"

Yuri put the wrench down, checked the tightened nuts, and nodded with satisfaction. "That's holding." Then he turned to his colleague. "From Tver, like your father and grandfather. Why do you ask?"

Andrei wiped his hands on a cloth and looked at his watch. "I'm hungry. Let's get something to eat."

Yuri followed. "I want a real answer this time."

"You gave it to yourself. We Ivanovs are all from Tver and were born in Tver. We live in Tver or the Oblast and have never left. The national player Oleg Ivanov was born in Moscow. It would be nice, but we're not related. At least not that I know of.

Almost a little disappointed that the opportunity to possibly get tickets to a European Championship game had disappeared at the same time as the answer, Yuri agreed. "Right, let's break for lunch."

92

They both left the hangar and went to the car. Their lunch was in the trunk of Yuri's Lada. Andrei stopped halfway. He pointed to the runway and gestured ahead. "See that?"

Yuri followed the outstretched arm of his colleague and friend. "There's nothing there. A bear."

Right next to the runway was a small bear cub.

"Where did he come from?"

Yuri looked around. "I don't know, but where the little one is, the mother is not far away. Let's go quickly to the car and get the food. We can watch from the tower as the mother fetches her runaway."

Andrei agreed. Both pilots went to the Lada. Yuri opened the tailgate and took out the basket with their lunch. Meanwhile, Andrei kept an eye on the young bear and heard his cries. "He needs help."

Yuri closed the tailgate. "What makes you think that?"

"Take a closer look. The little one isn't much bigger than a teddy bear. He's pawing desperately and calling for his mother."

Yuri picked up the phrase and added, "Who is about to come shooting out of the woods and attack us to save her young." He turned and headed for the tower. "Come now."

Andrei stopped. "Where should the mother be? I don't see any bear."

Yuri was slightly annoyed and put down the basket. "What are you going to do?"

Andrei shrugged? "I don't know?"

"Shall we eat then?"

Andrei hesitated. "He must be hungry?"

"Then why don't you give him some of your food," Yuri said annoyed.

Andrei had a different opinion. "That's a good idea. I'll go and see."

Yuri didn't want to believe it. "Are you crazy?"

The bear cub had approached to within a few meters while the two pilots were talking. He sat down on the grass and watched the two men. The frightened call came again and again. The wind played with the bear cub's hair. The cute animal was hardly bigger than a plush teddy bear. Andrei and Yuri looked again. There was no bear to be seen.

"There are poachers here too," Andrei said.

Yuri hesitated to answer. After a while he said: "Do you think the mother is dead?"

He shrugged. "Could be. Anyway, the little one is hungry."

Yuri looked at the bear cub, then at his friend. "How do you know that?"

Andrei frowned. "You have children," he hinted.

"Yes. But what does that have to do with anything?"

The obtuseness was incomprehensible. "My God, Yuri. It wasn't that long ago. When your daughters were little babies and hungry, what did they do?"

Yuri realized what Andrei was getting at. "Screamed."

"There you go," came the answer. At the same time, the call of the clumsy bear could be heard again.

Andrei plucked up courage. "We have watched long enough. It's time to act."

Boldly he reached into the basket and took out his bread. "Bears are omnivores."

Yuri thought for a moment. "When the mother comes, we have to get in the car and drive away immediately." At the same time, he tapped the outside of his pants pocket with his right hand and felt his key reassuringly. "You shouldn't let them get used to humans either," he added, but Andrei was already kneeling down in front of the little bear and handed him a sandwich with a spread.

The bear examined the human. He sniffed cautiously in the direction of the hand and the food. Andrei put the bread on the grass. The bear cub made a clumsy move forward and snatched the bread. It hungrily devoured the tasty morsel. Little by little, the pilot fed his lunch to the animal. With each bite, the little bear got closer to Andrei. It began to trust him and let him pet it. Less than five minutes later, Andrei was holding the bear cub in his arms. The animal cuddled up to him and felt safe. Thousands of thoughts went through Andrey Ivanov's mind. The feeling of holding a live wild bear in his arms was gigantic and incomparable to anything he had experienced before. He felt the cub seeking security, held it tightly and whispered: "It's all right, little one. I'll help you."

Andrei felt affection and responsibility for the bear cub from the very beginning. Yuri also petted the little bear and gave him some of his food. The rest he shared with his friend.

When the mother bear did not appear, the pilots suspected the worst.

"Did she fall victim to poachers?"

"Maybe. Or maybe she had an accident."

"Or a fight with another bear."

They waited another two hours, playing with the little bear. In the end, it was clear that the bear would probably not return. What fate it had suffered remained unknown. Gradually, other pilots joined them and surrounded the wild boulder.

When Andrej made the decision to continue helping the bear, everyone present agreed and wanted to support him.

Someone said, "He needs a name!" and after a few suggestions, he was given the name Mansur.

Within a very short time, the pilots at the Orlovka airfield built an enclosure for Mansur. It soon became clear that the little bear could not be released into the wild. He would not survive long without his mother. He was unable to hunt and was used to humans. He was fed by them.

After just a few days, it was clear that the bear would remain in human care.

"He will always want to be around people. We fed him," Yuri said.

Andrei agreed. "And that would lead to his death sooner or later. We don't need to have any illusions here. We rescued Mansur and took him out of the wild.

Calls to various zoos and conversations with hunters and veterinarians confirmed the pilots' suspicions.

Mansur stayed at Orlovka airport and quickly became the darling of all airport staff and passengers.

Andrei even took him on a flight once. The idea came to him when Mansur, full of curiosity, climbed into the open plane and made himself comfortable. But when the plane took off, the bear cub was no longer comfortable. He clambered up to the pilot, climbed onto his lap, and Andrei suddenly felt warm. Mansur was so scared that he wet his pants. After a few minutes Andrey landed again and from then on Mansur was spared any more sightseeing flights.

For Mansur, the airfield was a giant playground. He had toys everywhere, like hanging car tires or tree trunks, which were lying around or put together to make a climbing paradise. The little bear was everyone's friend and had access to almost everything.

In no time, he was nicknamed Airbear. Under this name, his fame quickly spread beyond the borders of the Tver region. Many people came to see and pet the bear. Mansur enjoyed it.

His best human friend was Andrey Ivanov. His best four-legged friend was a pilot's husky. He romped around with the dog and their friendship was unique.

In the early days, Andrei even took Mansur home with him from time to time. It started with the little bear not wanting to be alone when everyone went home in the evening.

"Why are you looking at me like that?" he would ask. The pilot looked into Mansur's wide-open eyes and pointed to the large fenced enclosure. "Look, there are still some apples lying around. You can enjoy them."

Mansur didn't even think about going into the enclosure. Instead, he trotted right up to Andrej and rubbed against the pilot's legs. Then he sat down and raised his paws. It looked like a small child begging to be picked up. He let out a low growl.

Andrei's heart melted. "All right, but just this once," he had given in.

In the weeks and months that followed, Andrei acquired an enormous amount of knowledge about bears. He scoured the Internet, devoured books, visited zoos, and talked to keepers and directors. He felt responsible for Mansur and was ready to take on that responsibility. He had a crucial conversation with a bear expert at the Moscow Zoo.

"Now the bear is small and cute, but he will grow. Mansur is a brown bear. He can grow up to three meters and weigh about 700 kilograms. Then he is no longer a cuddly toy. He can't retract the claws on his paws. It's a wild animal, not a pet."

Although Andrei knew all this, the words hit him like a punch in a boxing match. He knew he couldn't keep Mansur.

The bear expert continued. "Bears do not have facial expressions. That means you'll never know if he's in a good or bad mood. Even if he means well and swipes at you with his paw to show that he wants to be left alone, that swipe could be fatal."

Andrei swallowed when he heard the warning. "Do you know..." he paused, almost choking out the sentence. "Do you know of a good place for him?"

"Unfortunately, no. We have absolutely no place for your bear here."

Andrej got a lot of good advice and promised to take it to heart. As he drove back to the airport that day, he was sad. He knew that sooner or later he would have to say goodbye to Mansur.

The pilot enjoyed the next few weeks. He was with Mansur every day, introducing Airbear the tame giant to passengers and visitors.

Mansur grew and grew. The pilots at the airport thought back and forth about where to take their pet. Every zoo they approached turned them down. They advertised in the newspaper and on the Internet. Nothing. No response. They had almost given up hope when one day the phone rang. Yuri answered it, listened carefully and called his friend Andrei, who was working on an engine in the workshop.

"Andrei, there's someone who would take Mansur."

The sentence hit Andrei hard and yet with some relief. He immediately dropped the wrench, wiped his oil-stained hands on his trouser legs as usual, and hurried into the office.

Yuri closed the mouthpiece of the telephone receiver. "He says they have a reserve for bears."

Andrei picked up the phone. "Ivanov," he answered.

The caller introduced himself and said he was an animal lover. "...and that is why your bear cannot be released into the wild without help. It has been around humans for too long and would die or be shot by a hunter if it got too close."

The pilot had heard this sentence all too often.

"And you can help us?"

"Yes, I'm sure we can," the caller replied. "We are a group of bear lovers and we have set up a kind of nature reserve. There are bears here that would not survive in the wild without human help. We are always able to release some back into the wild, while others are allowed to live their lives in freedom in the large reserve."

"Freedom?"

"Compared to a zoo, yes. The area covers many square kilometers and is fenced in. Your Mansur can move around freely there."

"That sounds good, but how can I be sure that he's doing well there?" Andrej asked.

The caller laughed briefly. "I was waiting for that question. Of course you can visit Mansur at any time and see for yourself that he is doing well."

The last sentence had convinced the pilot. "That sounds good." He looked at his watch. "It's late. Can we talk on the phone tomorrow?"

"With pleasure. I'll call you around ten."

"Yes, that's fine."

Andrei hung up.

Yuri nodded in agreement. A smile spread across his face. He had overheard the conversation and patted his friend on the shoulder. "Looks like today is a sad happy day for us."

The day of parting felt bitter, and more than one pilot had a large lump in his throat. Mansur seemed to sense that something unpleasant was about to happen. No one really responded to his requests to play, and some of his things were packed up. Almost everyone was there to say goodbye to the Airbear.

When the old military truck pulled up to the airfield, Andrej wanted to cry and run away into the woods with Mansur, but he knew that this was the best thing for the bear.

In a nature reserve, Mansur could grow old without problems and enjoy his life without fear. The pilot's heart was beating faster than usual and he wiped away the first tears with the sleeve of his jacket. He sat down next to the bear and put down some apples for him.

"That's got to be it, old buddy," he said to his grown-up animal friend, stroking Mansur.

The truck pulled up and two men got out. The doors were slammed shut and the passenger had already made eye contact. "Andrei Ivanov?" he asked.

The friendly grin seemed artificial. Andrei sensed a certain reluctance, but chalked it up to having to say goodbye to an animal he had grown fond of. The man went to the enclosure. The other pushed aside the tarp of the truck bed. Behind it was a large, permanently installed cage.

"There's Mansur. I've read a lot about him," the animal rights activist said, holding out his hand to greet Andrej. His attention was focused on the bear, which he didn't seem to fully trust.

Andrej noticed the suspicious look. "Don't worry, he's really well-behaved and tame."

"Better safe than sorry," came the reply.

The expression was as cold and matter-of-fact as the handshake. "Take him to the cage. In my experience, the easiest way to hand him over and say goodbye is to get it over with quickly and leave immediately. The bear can also get used to his new surroundings in daylight."

Andrei picked up Mansur's blanket. "I'll give him this. He likes the blanket."

"Go ahead," he said with a smile, but cold eyes.

Andrei had a growing feeling that something was wrong, but he couldn't say what it was, so he led his bear to the truck. "Come on, you little rascal."

Mansur was very curious, so leading him to the truck was no problem. It was a welcome change for the bear to climb onto the back of the truck and take a closer look at the cage. He did not go inside, however, but cautiously stretched out his torso to sniff around. When Andrej threw the blanket in, Mansur stretched out with more than two-thirds of his body inside. The driver of the truck took a wooden pole lying next to the cage and hit Mansur's backside with it. The blow was not hard and was probably barely felt by the bear. It was the look on the man's face that made Andrei angry. "Hey, why are you hitting Mansur? It's not necessary."

The justification came immediately. "It was a very light push. He hardly noticed."

The second animal rights activist joined them. "Piotr only wanted to help." He saw that Mansur had now walked all the way into the cage in one step and closed the door. "You see, that was exactly the plan. Everything is fine."

Nothing is fine, Andrei thought. He felt more and more clearly that something was wrong.

Mansur turned and tried to open the door. He looked at his friend with big eyes. It was as if he wanted to ask Andrej for help. Get me out of here! Hey, I've been locked in by mistake. Why don't you help me?

The tarpaulin was closed and Andrej heard a humming noise. He had to go, and quickly.

"You know where to find us," the co-driver called, walking around the truck while the driver tied the tarpaulin. "Hurry up, Piotr." He got in, turned briefly to Andrei and said: "You can visit him anytime, but please make an appointment."

The truck was gone, Mansur was gone, and the small Orlovka airfield in the Tver region seemed to have become the loneliest place in the world. Everything was suddenly different. It was as if the heating system, which had been providing cozy warmth, had been turned off.

Andrei wasn't the only one who had a bad feeling about the supposed animal rights activists. Yuri and the other pilots also noticed a certain coldness radiating from both of them.

Andrei, Yuri and some of the other pilots hardly slept the following nights. They couldn't get the behavior of the animal rights activists out of their heads, and normal work was out of the question.

A few days later, as they sat together in a large group, Andrei spoke up. "As we have all noticed, we are not feeling well. I will call them and announce our visit. When we see that Mansur is doing really well and jumping around in the woods of the nature reserve, we'll feel better and we'll be able to sleep again."

Everyone agreed, so Andrey picked up the phone. He switched to listen in and dialed the number. It took a while and he was about to hang up when a woman's voice answered. She said her name and, somewhat unintelligibly, something about a nature conservation and training station.

Andrej introduced himself, asked how his bear was doing, and announced a visit.

Silence.

"Hello, are you still there?"

"One moment, I'll connect you."

Wait. After a minute or so, the familiar voice of the person who had come to meet us answered. "Good afternoon, Mr. Ivanov. Nice of you to call. What can I do for you?"

"I wanted to find out how Mansur is and to announce my visit."

"Well," said the man. "Your bear is doing very well. He's in the acclimation phase, and in our experience, it's very bad when he's in contact with his former environment. We strongly advise against it."

"You said we could visit him at any time."

"I told you that you'd need some time to get used to it."

Andrei became angry. The pilots listening in also looked at each other with questioning looks. "No! You didn't. I insist on visiting Mansur."

The animal rights activist's voice became a little friendlier. "We all want the best for the animals. Your bear is doing very well here."

"His name is Mansur!"

"Well, we've taken the humanization away from the bears to keep them as natural as possible. He's not a pet, he's a wild animal. He is a bear and he lives here like a bear."

"When can I visit Mansur?"

"Patience, Mr. Ivanov. Be patient. Your animal, uh ... Mansur, will be released into the wild. If you come here, you may not even get to see him. Our grounds are very large, and if he feels comfortable in the forest ..."

"He's fine, isn't he?" Andrej interrupted the animal rights activist.

"Of course he is. Don't worry about it. And thank you for calling. We'll keep you informed and get back to you as soon as the bear is settled."

Click

"He hung up."

Yuri slapped the table with the flat of his hand. "Something is really wrong!"

The other pilots immediately agreed. "What information do we have about this nature reserve?" came a not unfounded question from a female pilot.

"Guys, to be honest, I don't really have that much information. Mostly what that animal rights activist told me on the phone before.

Yuri stood up and walked over to the PC in the next office.

"We all did wrong here. None of us can be blamed individually, and there's no question that we'll take action now. I'll see what I can find out about this nature reserve."

An hour later, the pilots were certain that they had been duped. They had not given their Mansur to an animal rights activist, but to a hunting dog trainer. And to a hunting station that might be operating in a terrible way.

Although the training of hunting dogs to hunt bears on live animals has been banned in Russia since 2018, this cruel procedure is still practiced. Bears are chained, their claws are cut off and their teeth are pulled out so that they cannot hurt the dogs, and then the dogs are set loose on the defenseless, tormented bears. In addition to bears, this hunting dog training is also practiced on wild boar and other animals.

The Russian animal welfare organization helpni.ru, together with peta, is campaigning for animal welfare in Russia and has already written to the president demanding that the ban be enforced throughout the country. Unfortunately, footage from 2021 shows that dogs are still being chased after chained bears.

Andrei, Yuri and the others didn't think twice. Their decision was made.

"We're going to get Mansur out of there. Now!"

Half an hour later, they were in two cars, speeding away. Andrei hoped that nothing had happened to his Mansur. He would never have forgiven himself for that mistake.

The two cars sped along the bumpy highway. The drivers' nerves were on edge. How would they be received? Would the animal torturers fight back? Maybe even use weapons? Or could they set dogs on them? These and similar questions were hotly debated in both vehicles.

"These people are cold as ice. There is a lot of money at stake," Yuri exclaimed, regretting that he was unarmed.

Andrei replied in the negative. "They can't afford it. Mansur is the Airbear, and if he is tortured in violation of the new animal welfare laws, it will make the papers, cause bad press, and force the authorities to act."

"I hope your assessment is correct."

"And I hope Mansur hasn't been tortured yet."

The area looked more like an animal sanctuary than a nature reserve. The only thing reminiscent of conservation was the name of the hunting station, which referred to natural training. Whatever that might mean. Yuri thought of hidden clues to the ruthless, cruel training methods.

The two vehicles sped past the kennels and into a large courtyard. They saw the truck on which Mansur had been taken, parked next to it. The pilots got out. Andrei was full of rage. The barking of dogs accompanied him on the short walk to the office building.

Before they reached the door, the alleged animal rights activist came out of the building and stopped, startled.

"You cheater! I'm going to report you! Where is Mansur?"

The hunting station operator raised his hands in reassurance. "Relax, gentlemen. Your bear is fine. I promised you that. I just haven't been able to get him into the enclosure yet ..."

Andrej now stood in front of the man, standing up and leaving no doubt that he would not become violent. "Where is Mansur? And don't you dare harm a hair on his head. You are an impostor!"

The truck driver came around the corner, spotted the pilots, and immediately turned around.

"Stay calm. I'm not a cheater. We have a large area here. Come with me. I'll show you that the bear is fine," the guy tried to calm him down.

"So that's clear! We'll take Mansur back with us."

The supposed animal rights activist paused. "But I thought..."

Andrej moved very close to the animal abuser. They stood nose to nose. The pilot spoke very slowly and clearly. "I'm taking my bear now!"

The hunter swallowed nervously. His Adam's apple was moving up and down. "Of course. However, I would like to point out that you are leaving the bear to me to release into the wild ..."

"Shut up!" Yuri scolded from behind.

"We want our Airbear!" another pilot shouted.

The man raised his hands again in appeasement. "But of course. Take the bear back and the matter is settled. No problem at all. I'll take you to him."

Andrei and Yuri did not leave the man's side. He led them behind the house and to a cage. Mansur sat apathetically in a large cage. The pilots had never seen him in such a morbid mood.

"Mansur!" cried Andrei.
"Mansur," also came from Yuri.

The bear raised his head. He recognized his friends and stood up. There was a liberating roar. He knocked on the cage door with his powerful paws.
"Open up!"
"What if the bear..."
Andrei interrupted him again. "If you don't open the cage door right now, you'll wish it was the bear facing you and not me, because I'm about to break every bone in your body!"

With shaking hands, the man unlocked the padlock that held the door shut. As soon as the bar snapped up, he backed away. When he was a few feet away, he called out to the pilots: "Take the bear and get off my property!"

Yuri turned to the man and pretended to start running. The animal abuser then turned and ran into his office.

Mansur was beside himself with joy. He danced around, sniffed each of the pilots, and cuddled up to Andrey.

"Forgive me, I only meant well," he breathed to his friend.

Yuri patted Andrei's shoulder. "Now we've saved Mansur a second time. There won't be a third time. We'll take better care of him in the future."

"Let's get out of here," advised a female pilot. "I don't trust this guy."

They walked to the two vehicles and Mansur climbed into the trunk of the station wagon. Everyone laughed. The bear barely had room, but he laid down demonstratively. True to the motto. "Nobody can get me out of here!"

The joy was great. Mansur was actually still unharmed. It would have been unthinkable if his claws or teeth had been torn out. Andrei got goose bumps at the thought.

Back at the Orlovka airfield, Mansur was romping around and seemed to be catching up on everything he had missed over the past week. He was home and happy.

The next day, the small airfield crew celebrated Mansur's release. Their living mascot, the Airbear, was back. But they knew the bear could not stay with them. The search for a suitable place for Mansur began all over again. The crew started a second time, looking for a new home for their Airbear through newspaper ads, the Internet and some radio stations.

Mansur didn't notice any of this. He was happy. The bear played with his husky friend, was petted and fed by curious visitors, and wandered around the airport to watch the pilots at work or to play a trick and take something. The solution to the accommodation problem did not come by phone or e-mail. This time it was Yuri, who came to the airport office after a landing, beaming with joy.

"Say, why did you flap your wings like that on approach and now you shine brighter than the sun?" Sonja greeted him.

"I've just come from Oreshkovo airport."

Sonja was infected by Yuri's good mood. She grinned as she asked: "And that's where you found the golden suitcase, you're filthy rich and you're sharing with us."

Andrei joined them. "Well, you two lovebirds. What's the matter? Why are you in such a good mood?"

Yuri could no longer keep the secret to himself. "I have a place for Mansur."

Silence.

"A very good place," he added. "I've just returned from a flight to Oreshkovo in the Kaluga region. A businessman was going there. After landing, I took a break and talked to the air traffic controller there. I told him about Mansur and that we were looking for a home for him. Yuri took a break and unscrewed his thermos. He poured himself the last sip of tea and drank. The tension rose. "They knew our Airbear. Some of the people there have even visited him here before."

"Go on," Andrej urged excitedly.

"The air traffic controller gathered some pilots and they all offered to help immediately."

"That's nice, but how do you want to help us?" Sonja asked.

"Now comes the highlight. The airfield there also has its own fenced forest area. We can build a big enclosure for Mansur there. The place is a paradise. He can even roam through the forest."

Speechlessness was replaced by jubilation.

"That would be fantastic," Andrei clapped his hands.

Sonja hugged Yuri. "You did a great job!"

Andrej was moved to tears. Had his shaggy friend finally found a home? He patted Yuri's shoulders. "You are a true friend."

Yuri pointed outside. "He deserves it."

"He does," Sonja confirmed.

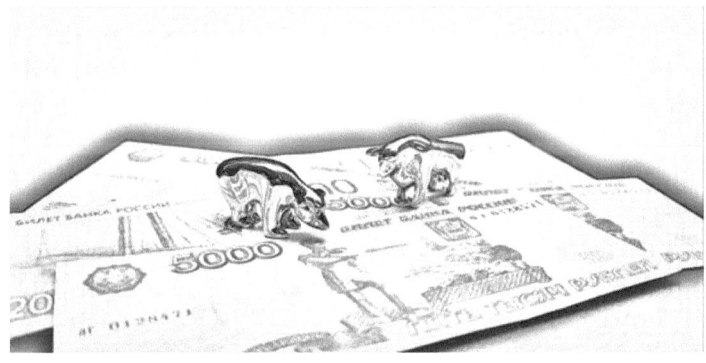

The next step was imminent. Money was needed to build a suitable enclosure for the bears. In addition to building Mansur's new home, his food had to be secured. His average food requirement was around €400 per month.

Fundraising appeals brought in the first cash and building materials were purchased. Many volunteers took part in the construction of the enclosure. A dream took shape.

There was no sadness on the day of the move. Andrej knew how well his bear would do in his new home. He was excited about the size of the enclosure and the opportunities for Mansur. Andrej also remained the bear's foster father and was able to visit him as often as he wanted.

Airbear quickly became a crowd pleaser and made many new friends in his new home. One of them had the great idea to make the bear an Internet star and earn his food money. The suggestion was accepted and Mansur has been featured on various platforms ever since. Advertising money and donations have been coming in regularly and his upkeep has been funded for the time being.

If Mansur continues to gain a large fan base, he will be set.

Andrej is still best friends with the bear he rescued as a cub. They spend as much time together as possible. In an interview, the pilot said that he would even like to build a pool for Mansur, depending on the amount of donations and advertising revenue he receives.

So the little bear who had lost his mother in an unknown way and was wandering around the Orlovka airport, helpless and hungry, found a loyal friend, a huge fan base and a place to live happily ever after.

Mansur's amazing story had a happy ending.

You can find more Laddy Stories on YouTube.

Tip: Subscribe to the channel and you won't miss a single story.

Laddy Stories

Licenses:

All photos and edited photos are from Pixabay:

Pixabay License: https://pixabay.com/de/service/license/

Many thanks to the photographers and to Pixabay.

Notice:

With the exception of pilot Andrei Ivanov, all names are fictitious. Any resemblance to real people is purely coincidental.

.